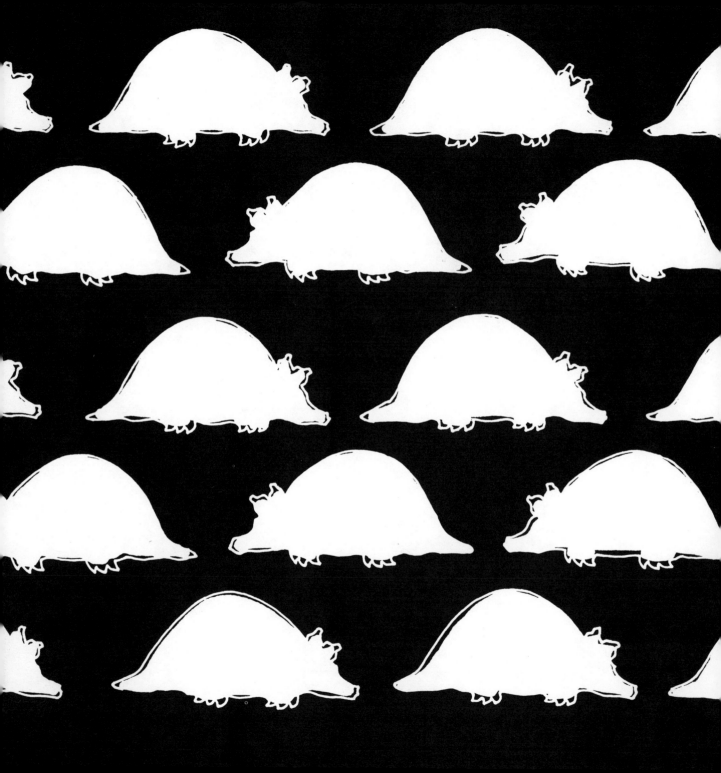

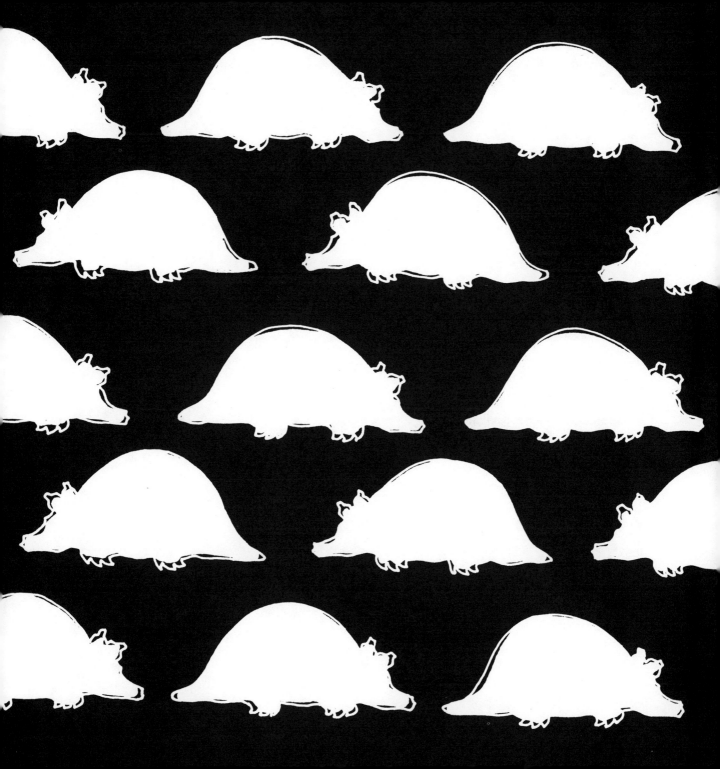

For my aunts and aunties: Ruth, Helen,
Jean & Christina; Betty and Doris; Ethelwyn, Muriel and Jocelyn
and
for my nieces and nephews: Sarah and
Kyla, Cyrus and Davin.
With special thanks to two Marys,
Jennifer and Mike.

Annick Press gratefully acknowledges the
support of The Canada Council and the
Ontario Arts Council

Canadian Cataloguing in Publication Data

Lewis, Robin Baird.
   Aunt Armadillo

ISBN 0-920303-38-2 (bound). - ISBN 0-920303-39-0 (pbk.)

I. Title.

PS8573.E93A97 1985   jC813'.54   C85-099294-X
PZ8.3.L48Au 1985

Distributed in Canada and the USA by:
Firefly Books Ltd.
3520 Pharmacy Ave., Unit 1c
Scarborough, Ontario
M1W 2T8

Printed and bound by Johanns Graphics, Waterloo, Ontario

Aunt Armadillo

ROBIN BAIRD LEWIS

ANNICK PRESS , Toronto

I want to tell you about a very special library,
but first you should meet my aunt.

Aunt Armadillo has a fantastic old home where
I love to spend my summers. It has dark, shiny
floors that are great to slide down. There are
cases of birds and animals, strange plants and
wind-up toys, ostrich feathers and silk fans,
opera glasses and a harpsichord, and rooms full of
thousands and thousands of books.

There are books about animals, books about
people and books about countries far away.
But best of all, there's Aunt Armadillo's
collection of hundreds and hundreds of
children's books.

While Aunt Armadillo might be writing another
letter to the editor about the aardvark at the zoo,
I love to read. In fact, we both read whenever we
want and go to sleep whenever we like, and
Auntie never asks me if I've made my bed.

We also eat whenever we like,
except at four o' clock it's always time for tea.
Then, after I've placed the armadillos carefully
on two pillows, we talk about all sorts of things
and sometimes argue about the books we are reading.

Nearby children sometimes call to play,
but they just want my red ball and they tease the turtle.

I much prefer to play with Auntie's armadillos.

Some nights we go on expeditions in the wilds of her garden.
We sing songs with the animals as we camp out around a little fire.

Some days Auntie is missing and I go to look for her in the library, the park or the zoo. I usually find her at the zoo, with Mr. Greene her neighbour, reading to the bears.

I love to listen to Auntie's explanations about where the animals came from and why they look the way they do.

Wherever we go, people stop and stare,
but we just ignore them.

In fine weather we love to go for a drive in Auntie's very old car.
Sometimes we even get to where we had planned to go,
if we follow my directions.

Other times we don't.
But we have so much fun it doesn't seem to matter.

On Sunday afternoons we go to the park
where Aunt Armadillo stands on a striped box
and reads a children's book to the crowds.

Mr. Greene applauds very loudly,
and I cheer and then we all go home.

One day last summer, a letter came from a library
asking Aunt Armadillo to come right away
and help look after their collection of very old
and very special children's books.

We were both very excited the next morning
as Auntie got ready. But I remembered, as usual,
to carefully dust and polish the armadillos.

Then, I waved goodbye to Aunt Armadillo
as she zoomed off to her first day on the job.

The library is not the same now that Auntie has made some improvements. She hung kites from the ceilings...

brought in a banana tree for her monkeys,
and piled all the wonderful children's books on the floor
to make them easier to reach. That's why Aunt Armadillo's
library is a very special place!

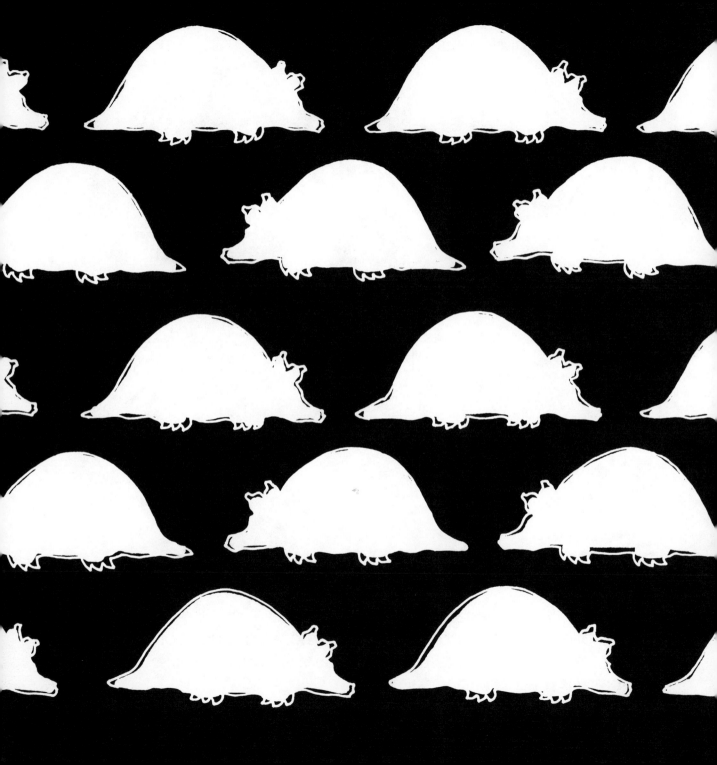

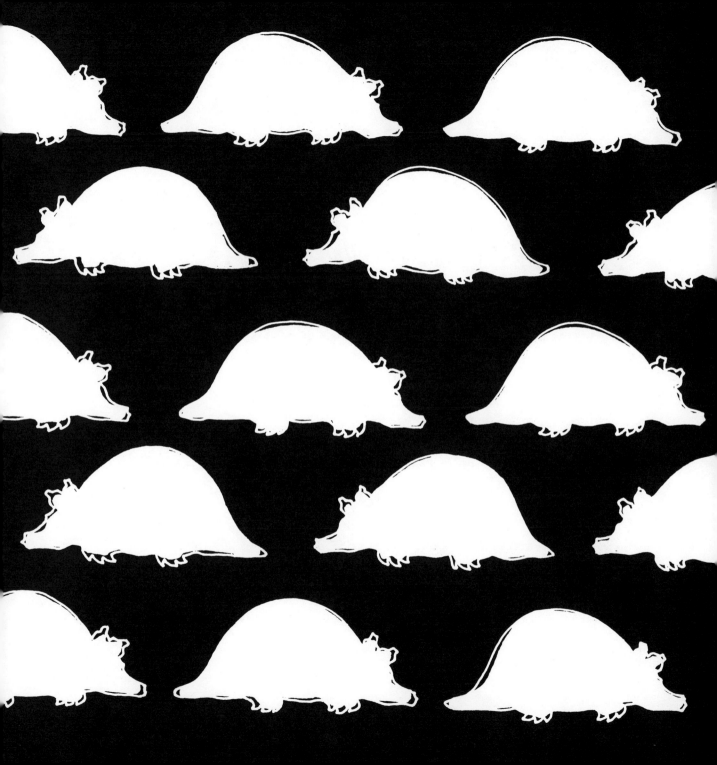